THE CASE OF
The Disappearing Beaune

A SHERLOCK HOLMES
CHRISTMAS MYSTERY

by

J. Lawrence Matthews

ISBN: 978-1-73667838-1 (Hardback)
ISBN: 978-1-73667835-0 (Paperback)
ISBN: 978-1-73667836-7 (eBook)
ISBN: 978-1-73667837-4 (Audiobook)

Library of Congress Control Number: 2022913927

Any references to historical events, real people, or real places are used fictitiously. All characters, incidents, and dialogue are drawn from the author's imagination and are not to be construed as real.

East Dean Press
Naples, FL

Dedication

For
Sarah and Claire

Born on September 3,
the date this book is being published.

I was going to quote a Dylan song here,
but the lawyers said no.
Then I decided
you both know the song anyway.

Love,
Dad

Disclaimer

The Case of the Disappearing Beaune: A Sherlock Holmes Christmas Mystery is an original work of fiction featuring Sherlock Holmes, John H. Watson, MD and other fictional characters introduced beginning in 1887 by Sir Arthur Conan Doyle. All such characters are now in the public domain and are used in the text of this book solely for the purpose of storytelling, not as trademarks. The personality traits of the characters depicted in this book are derived solely from those contained in the Sherlock Holmes books and stories in the public domain in the United States, not from the two stories which will remain outside the public domain in the United States until January 1, 2023.

This book is not sponsored or endorsed by or associated in any way with Conan Doyle Estate, Ltd. or any other party claiming trademark rights in any of the characters created by Sir Arthur Conan Doyle.

Jeffrey Lawrence Matthews asserts the moral right to be identified as the author of The Case of the Disappearing Beaune: A Sherlock Holmes Christmas Mystery.

Beaune [bōn] noun: a red Burgundy wine from the Côte de Beaune region of France.

I t was a cold, bright Christmas morning in the later years of my association with Mr. Sherlock Holmes when I called upon my old companion in his rooms at Baker Street to present him with the gift of a bottle of Scotch whisky and to invite him to join my wife and me at our home for a traditional Christmas dinner.

I had prepared my words of invitation carefully and with some trepidation, for I knew Holmes welcomed the solitude afforded by the holiday season. Criminal activity was always subdued at that time of year, and his landlady, Mrs. Hudson, often took the occasion to visit her family in the North of England. This left Holmes free to spend Christmas

Day alone with his chemical retorts and test tubes, working out some abstruse analysis whilst a fire in the grate warmed his rooms. When darkness fell, he would abandon his experiments, change into his evening clothes, and make his way to the Diogenes Club for a quiet Christmas supper with his brother, Mycroft Holmes.

I should hasten to point out that my friend's somewhat bohemian yuletide routine did not mean the significance of the occasion was lost upon him. Rather, he viewed society's embellishments upon its observance as an unnecessary artifice.

"Why, I give thanks every time I enter a church, Watson," he would say when, each Christmas, I encouraged him to leave his rooms and join me for dinner. "I hardly need to abandon my work on this particular day to be reminded of my blessings!"

And in all our years of friendship he had never once accepted my invitation.

But I was newly remarried after a long period of mourning following the death of my first wife, and my bride was determined that Holmes and his brother should abandon their habitual gathering at Mycroft's club to join us.

"I can think of nothing sadder," she said, "than the idea of two grown men eating their Christmas meal at some dreary old club in some dreary old dining room surrounded by dreary old men, without friends or children at their side!"

Deep down I agreed, of course, but I defended my friend's solitary nature and patiently explained the importance of those chemical experiments to his work in the field of criminal detection. My words did nothing to assuage her disapproval, however. Then and there she made it something of a mission to accomplish the seemingly impossible feat of relieving Sherlock Holmes of at least one of his habits.

So it was that I had left the house that morning with my gift for Holmes—and firm instructions to bring him home for dinner.

I let myself in at 221B Baker Street with my old latchkey and mounted the stairs to the rooms I had shared with Sherlock Holmes early in our professional association, all the while rehearsing my appeal one final time. After knocking thrice upon Holmes's door in my customary fashion, I entered.

At once my nose was met by the old familiar scent—a unique mixture of noxious chemical vapours, the sooty fragrance of a coal fire in the grate, and the sulphurous aroma of gunpowder, with a foul hint of stale tobacco smoke—that instantly brought back fond memories of our days together pursuing the outré cases which invariably came Holmes's way, nearly all of them somehow linking back to "that Napoleon of crime," as Holmes had often described his old adversary, the late Professor Moriarty.

When my eyes had adjusted to the dim light, I saw the familiar figure of my friend seated at the chemical table, still in his dressing gown and holding a delicate glass tube to his nose, cautiously sniffing at the neck.

"Ah! Watson! Do come in!"

Without glancing up from his glass tube, Holmes pointed to the fireplace with his free hand.

"Your Beaune is there upon the mantel, wrapped in some rather fanciful Christmas paper. I would hand it to you, of course, but this particular experiment is coming to a head, and I must see it through."

"Thank you, Holmes. And Happy Christmas." I found a space for the whisky bottle next to an ornate package atop the mantel and cleared my throat. "Mrs. Watson also extends her compliments and would be most pleased if you and your brother would—"

"Yes, yes," Holmes interrupted. "And do give your dear wife my deepest thanks, but as you can see, I am quite busily engaged at present."

"You haven't even asked what she has prepared for you!"

"Well, really, Watson, what difference would it make? You know I never leave my rooms on Christmas Day."

I shook my head, summoned my most aggrieved tone, and employed the alternative tack I had practiced all morning.

"Honestly, Holmes! You can be most trying at times! Margaret has gone to great lengths to accommodate you and your brother. There are *two* ducks in the oven and three pies already baked! The fire is lit and the places are set. It would be churlish indeed not to accept her invitation to join us in our first Christmas together as a married couple!"

Sherlock Holmes twisted around to face me, a kind smile upon his face.

"Yes, and I thank you, Doctor, but please tell the good Mrs. Watson that although you employed every brand of persuasion in your admittedly limited arsenal of guile, I remained unmoved, although not unappreciative."

As he turned back to his work, I sighed and picked up from the mantel the brightly wrapped package that was intended for me. It was quite a bit heavier than any wine bottle should be, and after removing the wrapper, I could see why. In place of the liquid contents, it had been filled with some sort of dark, coarse sand, while the cork had been replaced by a lace handkerchief stuffed into the neck!

Sherlock Holmes did not notice my preoccupation. He had resumed his inspection of the glass tube and seemed unaware I had not yet left the room.

"Holmes," said I, removing the handkerchief and peering down the neck of the wine bottle.

"Mmmm?"

"Holmes!"

He glanced up with an abstract expression.

"Ah, Doctor, please excuse me for failing to see you out, but the reagent has not had its intended effect, and I must—"

"No, Holmes, it's this bottle. Are you aware of what it contains?"

"Of course! It contains a most excellent pinot noir of the Gevrey-Chambertin region, from grapes of the *grand cru* estate—"

"More like *sand* from the *grand cru* estate, I should think."

Holmes gave a start and turned in his chair to face me.

"I beg your pardon?"

I removed the handkerchief from the neck of the bottle and stretched the lace fabric across my palm. Then, with my other hand, I held out the bottle and tilted the neck downward until several small clumps of moist sand dropped out onto the handkerchief.

"I believe that is *sand*, Holmes. Is this a practical joke of some sort on your part?"

Sherlock Holmes replaced the glass tube in its metal stand, carefully turned off the gas to the Bunsen lamp and rose from his chair, all the while gazing fixedly at the damp, dirty lumps of sand scattered across the lace fabric upon my outstretched palm.

"What the devil?"

Coming close, he peered at the stuff, then brought his nose almost into contact with one of the lumps and sniffed vigorously. Next, he took up a pinch between his fingers and studied the material for some few moments. Finally, he pulled a lens from the pocket of his dressing gown and examined the particles on the tips of his fingers by the light of the window, a look of wonder upon his face. Now he put away his lens, rubbed his fingers clean upon his dressing gown, and motioned for me to give him the bottle.

"I take it you did not intend to present me with a bottle of sand?" I asked, handing it to him.

"Not at all, Watson! This held a most promising red wine when I purchased it three days ago in the company of brother Mycroft. I daresay he'll vouch for that!"

Holmes carried the bottle to his chemical table, set it down, and rummaged among tin jars upon a shelf. Selecting a container of talc, he sprinkled the white powder all over the glass bottle, then trained his lamp upon it. Once more he whipped out his lens and now began studying every inch of the greenish-blue glass.

"No fingerprints, I perceive," said he, finally. "Save yours, of course."

"Well, I couldn't have known somebody had played a joke on us."

"Oh, this is no joke, Watson."

"Why do you say that?"

Ignoring my question, Holmes set aside his lens, tilted the bottle, and coaxed into the metal dish of his delicate scales a tablespoon of sand, which he carefully weighed. "Hmm!" Now he scooped up a thimbleful and tossed it into a glass beaker, adding a measure of water before turning on the gas and firing up the Bunsen lamp. Then he held the beaker over the flame, eyeing the sediment carefully. When the water had steamed off, a noxious smoke was released from the remaining mixture.

"I thought as much."

"What is it, Holmes?"

"This sand is of a unique type—one which I have almost certainly observed elsewhere in London. And quite recently, too."

There was that edge in Holmes's voice suggesting his little experiment had filled him with the heightened expectancy which came to my companion whenever a case of particular interest had found its way to his attention.

"You evidently think there is something more to this bottle of sand than, well, sand."

"Oh, I *know* there is, Watson."

He turned to his cabinet and opened a drawer filled with small test tubes containing the soil samples which he habitually collected from the various districts of greater London. After some searching, he removed a tube half full of dirt with a color remarkably like the sand retrieved from the Beaune bottle. He sprinkled some of its contents onto a thin glass slide, set a pinch of the material from the

Beaune bottle alongside this, then sandwiched the two samples beneath a second slender plate of glass. After fitting this assembly under his microscope, he carefully trained the light from the table lamp at it and put his eyes to the microscope for several minutes, muttering as he manipulated the plates with one hand and adjusted the focus with the other.

"Hmm. Yes. Hmm! No doubt!"

When at last he looked up, his eyes glistened with the steely intensity of a foxhound on the chase.

"Mrs. Hudson!" he shouted at the door. "MRS. HUDSON!"

"She is with her family in the North, Holmes. It is Christmas Day."

"Ah, yes, so it is. Well, that explains one small mystery, anyway."

"And what mystery is that?"

"Why, the mystery of the disappearing Beaune, of course! Surely you don't believe the vigilant Mrs.

Hudson would have let somebody steal inside her front door, climb the stairs to my rooms, and—while I slept—decant this bottle of Beaune and replace its contents with sand, then flee undetected?"

"I suppose not. Was there something very special about the wine, perhaps?"

Sherlock Holmes snorted. "As much as I appreciate your friendship, Watson, I should admit it was a good wine, but hardly worth stealing!"

"Why then replace it with this sand?" I asked, shaking out the dirty handkerchief over the grate. As I did so, the particles sparked and smoked in the heat. "Goodness, Holmes, did you see that?"

"I would have been surprised if the material *hadn't* flamed up, Watson!" said he with a chuckle. "I told you we solved one mystery today—well, therein lies the solution to a rather larger mystery."

"What might that be?"

"That of the sand itself." Holmes removed the glass slides from beneath the microscope lens and held them up for my inspection. "The manner in which those particles sparked indicates the presence of anthracite coal, which accounts for the bluish color of the sand in these two samples."

"What of it?"

"A quantity of anthracite coal was spilled recently upon a roadway in north-central London. When shoveled to the sidewalk to await disposal, it came to rest upon a sandy bed where a gas main is being laid. My little test tube contains a sample from that pile of dirty sand, and I have no doubt it is the same as we found in your bottle."

"That's quite a theory, Holmes!"

"It is no mere theory, Watson. It is conclusive. You saw the sparks fly! And, of course, I observed through my magnifying lens that the samples matched."

"But why would you have concerned yourself with a pile of dirty sand somewhere in London in the first place?"

"Because it resides outside the offices of a certain bookseller, a quiet, mousy-looking gentleman whom I strongly suspect has assumed the mantle of the late Professor Moriarty and now reigns over that vast criminal web which has engaged our attention so often in the past."

"Holmes, do you mean it?"

"Old friend Lestrade at Scotland Yard put me on the fellow's scent just last week, and I conducted an uninvited inspection of his premises the morning of my visit to the wine shop with brother Mycroft." He shrugged his shoulders. "It was not very revealing, of course. Great criminal minds are never careless, and for a public dealer in black-letter editions he is unusually secretive about his business. Nevertheless, upon departing I made certain that a quantity of the anthracite-laced soil outside his doorstep found its way into my pant cuffs, to supplement my little collection of London sediment."

"And you think this bookseller has paid you a visit in return?"

"Most certainly!" Holmes turned off the burner and replaced the test tube in his cabinet while speaking in his most didactic manner. "Consider the facts, Watson. I collect a small measure of sand from a distant corner of London one wintry afternoon, and three days later an entire bottle of the stuff appears upon my mantel. What else could it be but a message from one who sees himself as my adversary?"

"But why do you say the bookseller *himself* has done this and not one of his hired hands?"

"An underling might just as easily slit my throat while I was asleep rather than go to the lengths of stealing my wine and replacing it with sand! But whoever invaded my rooms had no desire to remove me from this mortal coil just yet. He wanted to leave a message… from one intellect to the other. Inference, it was the man himself."

"You evidently think this fellow is quite an adversary, Holmes. Who is he? And how did he rise so high in the criminal world?"

"One day you may learn something about him, Watson, but for now I lack sufficient evidence of my suspicions even to mention his name."

"What, then, do you propose to do?"

"I propose to relieve you of that dirty handkerchief and examine it for clues."

"Of course."

I gave the damp lace to Holmes, who spread it upon his knee and began to inspect it with his lens.

Almost at once, however, he jerked his head up with a start.

"Good God, man!"

"What is it, Holmes?"

Without answer, my friend leaped to his feet, stuffed the lens in his pocket and dashed into his bedroom, waving the handkerchief above his head and calling out over his shoulder.

"Hat and coat, Watson! We leave at once! And bring that wine bottle!"

W here are we going?" I asked when Sherlock Holmes reappeared, now dressed for the cold weather.

"To the Diogenes Club. We must alert my brother Mycroft."

He picked up his gloves and cap and held the door open for me.

"You think that handkerchief signals some danger, then?"

"I know it does," said he, urging me through the door and onto the stairs. "I don't quite understand why he left me an entire bottle of sand—any amount would have done. But that handkerchief is of significance."

"I don't see why. It was merely an object employed to stop up the wine bottle!"

"It is rather more than *that*, Watson."

"What makes you so sure?"

I have said that my companion finds it difficult at times to conceal his impatience with minds less keen than his own, and now was one of those times. He halted at the top of the stairs, and as I turned to face him, I found him holding up the square of lace fabric, his forefinger pointing to a tiny, delicately embroidered monogram in one corner.

"That is the mark of the former Prince of Wales—our newly crowned King of England," he said sharply. "And why an article from his private wardrobe was stuffed into a wine bottle left in my rooms is something we need to determine with all due speed."

Then he dashed past me down the stairs as a frantic ringing of the bell sounded. When Holmes opened the front door there stood a messenger bent over and gasping for breath, an envelope in his outstretched hand. Holmes grabbed the envelope, ripped it open and glanced at the message. Then he showed it to me without comment.

It read in this way:

Diogenes Club. Come at once. M.

Holmes pressed a coin into the hand of the still breathless young man and surveyed Baker Street for a cab, but traffic was light, so we began a brisk walk to the Marylebone Road, where he hailed the first hansom we saw and shouted the address as we climbed in.

"Fast as you can, driver!"

Soon we were off, and so speedily did we rattle over the cobblestones that conversation proved impossible. I hung on for dear life with the heavy, sand-filled bottle tucked safely inside my coat, while Holmes stared out the window, grim-faced and quietly marking our progress in his impatience to get there.

"Portman Square... Grosvenor Square... The Footman... ah! Here we are. The Diogenes Club. Thank you, driver."

"Bless you, sir!" said the fellow as Holmes handed up a half-sovereign before dashing away. "Happy Christmas, sir!"

But Holmes paid the man no attention, for soon he was engaged in a heated discussion with the young doorman in front of the club.

Mycroft Holmes, it seems, had been called away.

"Called away?" Holmes cried. "But I received a note from him at this very address not ten minutes ago!"

"Well, sir, I'm afraid Mr. Mycroft already left. And in quite a hurry he was."

"When was this?" Holmes asked skeptically.

It took a moment for the doorman, who was wearing a heavy coat and muffler against the winter chill, to retrieve his watch.

"It was an hour ago, sir. Exactly one hour—"

"Impossible! The messenger only just brought me this note!" Holmes waved it at the young man's face.

"I can't speak to that, sir. I can only tell you Mr. Mycroft departed an hour ago."

"And where was he bound?"

"Don't know the destination, sir." The young man nodded up the road. "But he went in that direction by cab." There came a nervous blinking to the doorman's eyes, and he seemed reluctant to say anything more.

"What is it, man?" Holmes said impatiently. "What are you hiding?"

"Well, sir, Mr. Mycroft was called away by... a woman."

"A *woman* came here for my brother? What sort of woman?"

"A very attractive woman, sir, if that is your sort of thing. Bright red hair, she had. Looked a bit on the rough side, if I may say so, but well enough put together, she was. Called here in great agitation, asking for Mr. Mycroft. Said she had information only he could understand."

Sherlock Holmes put a gloved hand to his chin in wonder.

"That sounds like Miss Kitty Winter, does it not, Watson?"

"It does indeed," said I.

Kitty Winter hailed from the lower reaches of London society and had played an important role in helping us with several of our most notorious cases, including that of Baron Adelbert Gruner, the Austrian socialite murderer. It had been some time since we crossed paths with her, but one could never forget the striking figure, the fiery demeanour, and the flaming red hair.

"She came alone?" Holmes asked the doorman. "No companion with her? A large, red-faced man with very black eyes, perhaps?"

Holmes was describing Shinwell Johnson, a close companion of Miss Winter and an informant in his own right who moved easily among the criminal classes, having been a rising star in their peculiar firmament before drink and ill health caused him to reassess his career and make Holmes's acquaintance. Along with the "Baker Street Irregulars" (Holmes's affectionate name for the street urchins who provided his eyes and ears in the by-streets and back alleys of London during our early years together), Miss Winter and Mr. Johnson had been by far the most important links in my friend's sturdy chain of informants.

But the doorman shook his head.

"Alone, she was."

"Alone? Why would she have come on her own for brother Mycroft?" Holmes asked himself. "Why not come to me first?" He glanced sharply at the doorman. "Well? Did you hear nothing of her errand?"

"Not exactly, sir."

"'Not exactly, sir'! What then? What did you overhear? Was it something about a 'Beaune,' perhaps?"

"Beg your pardon, sir?"

"A Beaune, man! A disappearing *Beaune*."

"Why no, I heard nothin' about a missing bone, sir. It's a dog you're after, then?"

"No. No. No." Sherlock Holmes buried his face in one hand and slowly shook his head. When he had recovered himself, he placed his nose inches from the doorman's. "There was *no* dog. There was *no* bone. It was a *wine* that's gone missing—but never mind that. Just tell me what the woman said."

The poor fellow appeared greatly agitated and glanced back at the club's entrance, as if worried he would be overheard.

"Come, come, what *was* it, man?"

"I'm sorry, sir, but it is against club rules to repeat information overheard during the conversation of a club member," said the doorman, reciting the relevant bylaw he had evidently learned by heart.

"You know who I am?" Holmes asked sharply.

"Yes, sir. Of course, sir. Mr. Sher—"

"And you know that Mycroft Holmes is my brother."

"Yes, sir, but the rules—"

"Do the rules govern your conduct if my brother, *the* club member, is involved in a matter of life or death?"

The doorman blinked. "I'm sorry, sir. Of course not. What I heard was, I heard them say something about a 'Lestrade.'"

"Lestrade!"

"Yes, sir. Mr. Mycroft said they must 'take it to Lestrade.'"

"What happened next?"

"Well, this red-haired woman gets very excited, like, and backs away from him. Says she won't go."

"And what did my brother do?"

"He tells her, 'If you don't come with me to Lestrade, my good lady, I'll have you in the dock on Boxing Day!' And off they went."

Holmes nodded. "Very well. Mycroft and Miss Winter made for Scotland Yard. Thank you, my good man."

But the fellow refused Holmes's offer of a tip.

"Club rules, sir. I thank you all the same, sir."

Sherlock Holmes shrugged his shoulders and turned on his heel.

"Come, Watson."

Once more, however, there were no cabs available, and so we began the walk down St. James's Street in the direction of the Yard, Holmes sunk in the deepest thought.

It was I who called attention to the mysterious carriage following us.

The rather fine-looking brougham had been standing idle outside the Carlton Club as we passed by that establishment, but soon the driver started it up at a slow pace, pausing each time I glanced backward. As we turned into Pall Mall, the brougham also made the turn.

It was then that I nudged my friend.

"Holmes, we are being followed."

"And what of it?" he said, continuing at a brisk pace, his mind upon the task at hand. "Since my return from the Continent following Moriarty's fatal plunge at the Reichenbach Falls, I am watched wherever I go."

"But shouldn't we *do* something?"

Holmes chuckled grimly and shook his head.

"If he's like the other poor bunglers they send after me, he'll soon develop a thirst and stop at the next pub. I think we owe it to His Majesty to get to Scotland Yard with all due speed."

"But *this* 'poor bungler' is driving a gentleman's carriage!"

My companion started.

"A carriage?"

"Yes, and he's been following us ever since we left the club."

"Well done, Watson," said Holmes without turning his head or pausing in his stride. "Can you describe the man?"

"Not well. He's wearing a cap pulled down to his eyes, and almost certainly the beard is false."

"Does he know you have spotted him?"

"I think he does."

"Then it cannot be helped. In any case, we'll soon be at the Yard." Holmes quickened his pace. "This is evidently a crisis of national importance."

"Why do you say that?"

"You know that our new king was crowned less than four months ago?"

"Yes, Holmes, I *do* follow the news," I said with some asperity.

"Can you think of a better time to instigate a threat to the Crown than when a new and untested head of state wears it?"

"Perhaps not. But how does a bottle of dirty sand and the King's stolen handkerchief signify a 'threat to the crown'?"

"You still don't see it, Watson?"

"No."

"Well, I don't pretend to hold *all* the strands of this mystery, yet, but whatever Kitty Winter heard that has commanded the attention not only of Mycroft Holmes, who represents His Majesty's Government, but Inspector Lestrade of Scotland Yard, it cannot be a trivial matter! And when a handkerchief makes its way from the King's holiday retreat at Sandringham to my sitting room in London at the same critical moment... why, it becomes positively momentous, don't you think?"

"But supposing the appearance of the handkerchief is just a coincidence? Perhaps it was found by chance in some London boudoir by this bookseller or one of his agents? The King did have a reputation for rather indiscreet assignations when he was Prince of Wales, did he not?"

"He may have had that reputation, Watson, but he is undoubtedly our new head of state, and however the handkerchief was acquired, I think the message in that bottle is clear enough. There is danger to the King, and our nondescript bookseller is behind it all."

"But why on earth would he have left *any* clue in your rooms? Why not act first and take the credit later?"

"Bravo, Watson. I have been wondering that myself. I rather think he *had* intended to act first, but his plans were disarranged by the appearance of the good Kitty Winter at my brother's club this morning."

"Why did she go to Mycroft instead of you?"

"That, also, I have been wondering, and I think I have worked it out. Miss Winter now inhabits a rather more refined circle of acquaintances than when last we encountered her, if you catch my meaning," Holmes said, raising an eyebrow. "I have no doubt she is known to several members of the Diogenes Club—not Mycroft, of course, but she would certainly be aware of his standing at Whitehall thanks to her other... *friends* there. And if this plot involves our new head of state, why, she has brains enough to realize it is Mycroft Holmes who must immediately be informed, not his brother."

"Why would she resist going to Scotland Yard with Mycroft?"

"The answer to that is rather more obvious. You recall Miss Winter spent some little time in prison for that vitriol-throwing incident involving the detestable Baron Gruner? Then I think you can understand why she would shy from another encounter with the official police!"

"I suppose you are right, Holmes."

My companion now glanced behind us as we crossed Parliament Street.

"And so have you been, Watson. We *are* being followed, and not by one of the dull fellows I've become accustomed to seeing on my heels. No— don't turn. Just keep walking. Whatever is planned for the King at Sandringham must be stopped. We cannot be distracted from our task."

"But why go first to Scotland Yard? Why not make directly for Sandringham?"

"Because it may not be the country that Mycroft and Lestrade are bound for. You yourself indicated that the King's appetites took him rather far afield from his official duties. He could be anywhere, in town or at Sandringham."

"How will we know where they have gone?"

"An inspector of Lestrade's rank is on call every hour of the day, even a holiday such as Christmas, and precisely for occasions such as this. Once I have determined where he signed himself out for the next few hours, we can follow. Here we are, Watson. New Scotland Yard."

It was a tall, stately building in the Georgian style, newly opened the previous year. Before entering, my companion turned briefly and gave the driver of the brougham an insolent wave.

Then we disappeared inside.

The sergeant at the desk seemed a bit flustered at the appearance of Mr. Sherlock Holmes on Christmas Day, but he answered Holmes's questions without hesitation.

Yes, Inspector Lestrade had been called to the Yard—by a rather portly fellow in the company of a redheaded woman, about an hour ago. Then? Well, the woman told her story to the Inspector and was dismissed. Next? Why, there was a brief discussion of the railway timetables before Inspector Lestrade and the portly fellow departed by cab. No, the sergeant didn't hear what was discussed. Yes, of course, Mr. Holmes could inspect the time sheet!

The sergeant twisted the book around on the desk, and my friend cocked his head and glanced at the notation next to Lestrade's signature. Then he nodded, thanked the sergeant, pushed the book back across the desk, turned on his heel and strode out the doors.

The brougham was nowhere to be seen.

"So, where did Mycroft and Lestrade go, Holmes?"

"St. Pancras Station. The 1:15 train bound for Sandringham."

"We have thirty minutes, then. Might we want to pick up my service revolver on the way?"

Holmes glanced at his watch and considered this for a moment.

"Yes, it's at most ten minutes to the station and your house is not so far out of the way that we would miss the train—provided the gun is readily at hand?"

"Locked in my desk and newly cleaned."

"Excellent, Watson!"

"And here is a cab," said I as one pulled up. Holmes, however, waved it on. "Why did you send that cab away?" I asked as the hansom drove off. "Surely you don't think there's time enough to *walk* to my house?"

"Surely not, Watson, but I rather think we must be more careful from here on. Our adversary plays a deep game. That cabby was waiting for us."

"Indeed!"

Holmes nodded grimly and waved away the next cab as well. Spotting an idle hansom on the other side of Parliament Street, he crossed, and I followed. The driver, a bearded man in a cape, was adjusting the bridle on his horse. Holmes slapped a gleaming sovereign upon the mare's back and, without awaiting an affirmative answer, shouted my address. The man snatched up the coin and jumped onto the box as we climbed in.

I had barely taken my seat when the cab abruptly lurched into motion, made a sharp turn in the proper direction, then proceeded at a brisk trot up Parliament, passing by Downing Street while making for Trafalgar Square.

Sherlock Holmes sat back in the cushions and stared out the window muttering to himself.

"But why an *entire bottle* of sand…?"

We whirled through Trafalgar Square and were flying up the Charing Cross Road when the traffic suddenly halted. A coal wagon was stopped outside the old Morland Hotel, making its delivery. As we idled, our hansom was approached by a woman in

Salvation Army uniform collecting for the poor. Holmes impatiently dropped a coin in the jar and slumped back in his seat, but his attention had been drawn to the flag of Denmark flying above the entrance to the hotel, which in those days housed the Danish Club of London.

Gathered beneath the flag could be seen the woman's compatriots, singing a Danish Christmas carol. They were quite good, being led expertly by a costumed, white-bearded Santa with a clear, beautiful tenor voice.

Suddenly Holmes sat bolt upright.

"Is your cap precious to you, Watson?"

"I beg your pardon?"

"Your cap. I perceive you did not wear your best this morning."

"Well, no. Margaret thought my old faithful was getting a bit ragged, so she brought it to the shop for mending. I found this one instead." I removed the battered felt cap and studied it rather ruefully. "You're concerned I won't look presentable at Sandringham?"

"No. I'm concerned about what's inside that wine bottle!" Holmes took my cap and placed it upside down on the floor of the cab, then stretched out his hand. "Now, the bottle, Doctor."

I removed the heavy object from my inner pocket and placed it in his hand. But instead of examining it with his lens, as he might have been expected to do, Holmes turned the bottle over, pointed the neck at my cap upon the floor and began shaking it violently. Dirty clumps of sand dropped into the cap between our feet as the cab started up again.

"What are you doing, Holmes?" I cried, holding on as the cab shot up Charing Cross Road.

He ignored my question and continued shaking out sand until a quantity had been released. Then he stopped and peered into the neck.

"Hmm!"

Once more he turned over the bottle and resumed his frantic efforts, spilling out the contents like a child, without any regard as to the consequences to my poor cap.

"Holmes! May I ask what you are doing?"

"The sand, Watson! The sand!" he cried, once more righting the bottle and staring into the neck. "What else is in this bottle besides *sand?*" Then, shaking his head in disgust, he resumed his attack upon my poor cap.

Holmes continued in this fashion, alternately emptying the bottle and peering inside it as the cab continued its journey, until the pile rising from my cap had grown several inches high and the contents within the bottle had diminished to no more than a tablespoon.

Finally, he gave the bottom of the bottle a good thump with his free hand, causing a small, dirty item in the shape of a slender bean to pop out of the neck and onto the mound of sand.

After handing me the empty bottle, Holmes picked up the object in triumph, rubbed it clean, and held it to his eyes.

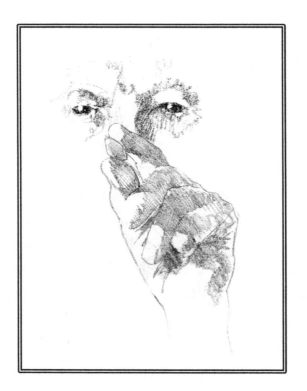

"I knew it, Watson!"

"What is it?"

"The prize! The prize! I knew I'd find it!"

"Not much of a prize," said I, shrugging my shoulders. "It looks like a dirty almond."

"It *is* an almond. *The* almond. From the *Risalamande!*"

"The riss-ala-what?"

"The Risalamande. Rice pudding, the traditional Danish Christmas dessert. A single almond is mixed with the pudding, and whoever finds the almond in their serving gets an extra helping."

"And you thought you might find one in the bottle?"

"I *knew* I would find it. Once I saw the flag and heard that tenor singing the old Danish carol, I remembered."

"Remembered what?"

Holmes fixed his eyes upon me and spoke with peculiar gravity. "Alexandra, the former Princess of Wales, and now Queen Consort, is a *Dane*, Watson."

"Why, you are right, Holmes! But what does it mean?"

He placed the small object in his watch pocket and resumed his gaze out the window, his face a mask of concern.

"It means, I fear, that the threat is not reserved for the King only," he said, slowly and severely. "It means an attack upon his entire family. Perhaps upon the very line of succession."

"How can we stop it, Holmes?"

"By getting your revolver and making the 1:15 from St. Pancras."

Our cabman, however, had other ideas.

The hansom was now racing along Tottenham Court Road and Sherlock Holmes had resumed mouthing the names of each by-street when I noticed him suddenly tense up. We had not yet reached Howland, the main thoroughfare leading to my street, but the cab was already slowing down.

Holmes banged on the ceiling.

"Not here!" he shouted. "Don't turn here!"

But it was too late. The cab made a sharp turn into a narrow alley.

"Goodge Street?" Holmes cried. "Why are you taking Goodge? It's a by-street! We'll never make it in time."

The cabby ignored Holmes's shouts. Instead, he made the next turn, then another, and now we were flying down Tottenham Court Road in the wrong direction!

"Brace yourself, Watson! This fellow is not our friend. We'll have to jump for it at the next opportunity."

Holmes grabbed the door handle and pulled himself forward, crouching. Soon enough the cab halted abruptly in traffic, and in that instant, Sherlock Holmes threw open the door and leaped out. I followed, cradling the empty wine bottle inside my coat, just as the cab suddenly started up again.

"Shall we pursue him, Holmes?" I cried, watching the hansom rattle away. "I have the bottle as a weapon!"

"No, that is precisely what he wants us to do. He wants us to miss that train."

"Then… what?"

"We find another cab. But this time we'll employ rather more discretion than the last."

Holmes waved down the next hansom that came along, but instead of climbing in, he held the horse's bridle and spoke sharply to the cabman.

"For whom do you drive?"

"McKenna's, guv!" responded the man, appearing somewhat startled behind his thick beard and long mutton whiskers. "Why d'you want to know?"

"Where are your stables?"

"Vincent Square!"

"What's the fastest horse in the stables?"

"Beg pardon, sir?"

"The fastest horse at McKenna's. What's its name?"

"Why, that would be Khartoum, sir. Why'd you want to kn—"

"Never mind. You'll suit our purpose."

He gave the cabman my address and we climbed in.

"I visit McKenna's whenever I need a fast horse," Holmes explained as the cab started up. "Khartoum is by far his best mount. This fellow is all right."

"I suppose the other cabby was in league with the bookseller?"

"Of that I have no doubt. I'm not often impressed, Watson, but that quiet little man plays a very deep game indeed. Knowing my habitual caution and arranging *three* cabs to greet us outside the Yard, when I thought I was being careful enough by rejecting the first two!"

"You mean to say this entire journey—"

"Anticipated by the bookseller, yes," said Holmes, checking his watch. "The same fellow who replaced the wine with sand, added that fine touch of the almond in the 'pudding,' and plugged the neck with the King's own handkerchief. He evidently means to keep us from arriving at St. Pancras on time. But we will, Watson. By the Lord Harry, we will. And armed with your revolver!"

The cab turned into my street and Holmes ordered the driver to slow his pace while he instructed me on how to handle my brief visit home.

"Make it quick, Watson, but do not alarm your wife. Pretend all is well, but don't remove your coat— you'll need to make a hasty exit after securing your gun."

"But how shall I explain my leaving so quickly?"

Holmes considered this for a moment, then nodded at my bare head.

"My exertions with the wine bottle help us there. You'll explain that you left your cap behind in the cab and must fetch it. Do *not* tarry even for a—"

Holmes stopped speaking and gazed fixedly down the street to where my doorstep was visible a hundred yards or so away. As I followed his gaze, I let out a hoarse yell.

The elegant brougham that had followed us to Scotland Yard stood just outside my door, and a woman with flaming red hair was being pulled from the carriage by the driver with the false beard! The blackguard appeared to wrestle her to the door, then both disappeared inside, the red-haired woman giving a last wave of her arms in evident distress.

I immediately sprang from the cab, coming down hard upon the sidewalk.

"No, wait!" cried Sherlock Holmes, following me out of the cab. "Stay yourself, Watson!" I had raised myself to make a dash for the house when Holmes's strong hand gripped my arm and held me back. "This is not the time to act in haste."

"But the fiend has entered my house!" I shouted, struggling against Holmes's powerful grip.

"Yes, but I am almost certain his aim is not to bring harm to your wife."

"How can you know that? Let go of me, Holmes!"

"Steady on, Watson. Consider the facts. That fellow entered by the front door with the unfortunate Miss Winter *in full view of us*. Why? He wishes to draw us in after him. I told you my bookseller plays a very intelligent game, and this is all a part of it."

"Whether he wants me by the front door or not, that's where I'm going! Leave go of my arm!"

"Please, Doctor. This is no time for rashness."

"Time enough, Holmes! My *wife* is in that house!"

"Yes, and so is a brute in the employ of one of the most dangerous men in this city. We must use our wits, not our fists."

I slackened my efforts at freeing myself from Holmes's grip.

"That's better, Watson. Yes, the more I think of it, the more I'm convinced that scene upon your doorstep was designed to prompt a rash move on our part."

"But what, then?" I cried, my voice trembling with frustration. "What do we *do*?"

"First, we summon the police." Holmes thrust a gold sovereign into the hands of the waiting cabman, who had been looking on in evident consternation from beneath his low cap. "Fly at once to Scotland Yard! Tell the sergeant at the desk what you have seen and heard here! *Now!*"

As the hansom clattered away, Holmes drew me into the shadow of the nearest doorway, from which he studied the scene several doors down, all the while keeping a grip upon my sleeve.

"What are you doing, Holmes?"

"What I should have been doing all along, Watson. Observing."

He carefully surveyed the passing traffic, which was light, then craned his neck at the houses nearby.

"Well?" said I impatiently.

But Holmes shook his head. For the first time in my many years by his side, I witnessed perplexity emanating from his every word and gesture.

"I don't understand it, Watson. Why your house? If the bookseller seeks merely to cause us to miss the train, surely *any* diversion would have sufficed. And why Kitty Winter? If both Mycroft and Lestrade have already heard her story, what need would there be to kidnap her? I should think all his efforts would have gone towards preventing Mycroft and Lestrade from catching that train. Unless…"

"Unless what?"

"Unless his goal in this little chess match is to eliminate my powers of reasoning altogether before carrying out whatever he is planning for the Royal Family at Sandringham."

"But why would he try to stop *you*, and not Mycroft? You've often said that your brother's powers of deductive reasoning are far greater than your own."

"Indeed, they are, Watson." Holmes suddenly relaxed his grip, and a twinkle came to his eye. "But not by much!"

"You see a way, then?"

"There is a mews behind these houses, is there not?"

"Yes."

"And your kitchen, I believe, opens into the mews?"

"Yes, but why, Holmes? You expect this fellow will try to flee out the back?"

"No, his carriage is tied up out front—I hardly think he will depart through the kitchen. Rather, I expect *you* will *enter* that way."

"But why should I enter by the kitchen? He has gone in the front door!"

"Precisely. He wants you to follow him that way. He knows your instinct for action. You believe your wife is in peril and you will naturally charge straight inside. Therefore, you must do the opposite. You will enter by the rear—and you will make certain he hears you doing it."

"To what end, Holmes?"

"To this end: while *you* appear to be attempting to outfox the brute by entering through the rear of the house, *I* will be making my way by stealth through the front to take him unawares. You have a latchkey to your door? Give it to me. Thank you."

Holmes stuffed the key into his pocket and glanced at his watch. Then he put his hand upon my shoulder and gazed with the piercing grey eyes that told me he had recovered his masterful self.

"It is five minutes to the hour, Watson. Make your way around by the mews to your kitchen, but not so quietly that your deception fools the ruffian! Peer in through the barred window, bang into the dustbins, rattle the door latch. Make yourself known! Then, exactly upon the hour, open the door—with your shoulder if it is latched! That will be my signal to enter by the front, and we will have him!"

He squeezed my arm and gave me a knowing smile.

"Mrs. Watson will be unharmed, I can assure you. It's me they want."

I could hardly disagree.

Some few minutes later I was in the mews, banging around the dustbins and peering in at my kitchen window in accordance with Holmes's instructions. Finally, I tested the door and found it would not need to be forced open—although, in truth, I had never intended to break into my own kitchen.

I knew the door would be unlatched.

One minute before the hour I simply let myself in.

Pressing a finger to my lips as the cook glanced up from the oven to greet me, I moved silently past the kitchen table groaning with platters piled high with boiled vegetables and roots of all kinds; a serving tray with one of the two ducks she had just removed from the oven; and three pies still cooling by the window. At the dining room door, I paused and listened, then gently pushed it open.

To my great satisfaction I saw the room was filled with the friends and relations who had gathered to share Christmas dinner with Mr. Sherlock Holmes.

There were Kitty Winter, of the flaming red hair, and Shinwell Johnson, now stripped of the thick black wig of the brougham driver, both enjoying their punch together and looking no worse for the little scene they had enacted upon my doorstep.

There were the half-dozen former Baker Street Irregulars—now shorn of the heavy mufflers, wigs, and caps with which they had disguised themselves during their cab driving and doorman and messaging duties—and their wives, still in Salvation Army costumes, and all with smiles upon their faces as they regaled Inspector Lestrade and Mycroft Holmes with the tale of how they had managed to pull one over on their esteemed old taskmaster, Mr. Sherlock Holmes.

And there was my wife, looking as happy as I had ever seen her, knowing that my friend and companion would indeed be sharing our Christmas Day meal.

I caught the expectant eye of Mycroft Holmes, standing tall and portly next to the diminutive but stout Lestrade, and signaled that all was ready. Mycroft took his position at the door to the front hall, making sure it was closed just enough to hide us all from view, and my wife tapped a glass and held a finger to her lips to quiet our guests.

A hush fell upon the room.

Exactly upon the hour a distinct metallic snick came from the front doorlatch, and another minute later the faint creaking of a hallway floorboard sounded in the passage. Everyone took in their breath when a slight tremor of the dining room door could be seen, indicating that our unsuspecting guest had cautiously gripped the handle. And when at last the door was thrown open, we all beheld the astonished face of Mr. Sherlock Holmes.

There was, at first, confusion in his eyes, then the sudden realization of all that had been done to bring him to our dining room, and finally embarrassment as a crimson flush overcame his pale, austere features.

In that instant, I felt a deep regret for my actions. Even shame.

How could I have been so wrong?

To have embarrassed my old companion in front of all these friends! In my own house! And on Christmas Day!

I berated myself in silence.

I t had been at my wife's instigation that the plot had been carried out, of course. And I could not deny that Mycroft Holmes had enthusiastically approved her notion, although he had doubted from the outset that his brother could be as thoroughly fooled as the expression upon my dear friend's face now indicated. Nevertheless, Mycroft had taken up his part with delight, devising and staging the elaborate ruse that had delivered Sherlock Holmes from the perfect contentment of the chemical table to this gathering of which it plainly appeared he wanted no part.

Nor had any of the other participants expressed a reluctance to do their share, I might add. Quite the opposite, in fact!

To a person, they had been overjoyed at the prospect of being able to demonstrate in some small measure the esteem and affection with which they held this supremely dedicated man whose singular career in the detection of crime had enriched the lives of every one of them—from the hardened criminal-turned-law-abiding-informant Shinwell Johnson and his loyal accomplice, Kitty Winter, to the orphan boys Holmes had rescued from the streets of London and molded into his "Baker Street Irregulars," to a once-up-and-coming young Scotland Yard detective now known as the august Inspector Lestrade.

But whether the ghastly expression upon the face of Sherlock Holmes sprang from embarrassment that he, the self-possessed master of observation and deduction, had been utterly fooled in that department, or from mortification at the presence of so many individuals to whom he would be expected to exhibit the good graces and proper manners of the season when, in truth, he would rather be alone in his rooms pondering those chemical experiments he cherished—or something of both—it was quite obvious to me that his reaction to our scheming was not been what I had anticipated.

Nor would it in any way suit the spirit of the season.

The laughter had died in our throats and the good cheer in the room entirely vanished. I cleared my throat and was about to bring the proceedings to a hasty end when the startled round eyes of Sherlock Holmes gave way to a somber countenance, and he motioned me not to speak. Just then I felt my wife's hand curl around mine and squeeze it in the encouraging manner of a spouse who knows when a hard truth is to be revealed to her mate, and he needs to know that he is not alone to face it.

But at that very moment a crinkled looked of merriment entered Holmes's eyes, and the open-mouthed expression of shock upon his lips was replaced by a wide smile. Then he clapped me upon the shoulder and began to laugh such a laugh as I had never heard from my oldest and dearest friend.

Now we all laughed, and tears of relief filled my eyes as one by one every person in that room greeted Mr. Sherlock Holmes with the compliments of the season, using expressions of the utmost respect and deepest affection.

And those affections were returned by Holmes, albeit in his own stiff and rather demure manner, to each in turn.

But his greatest warmth, I am pleased to say, was reserved for my wife.

L
ater, after we had been seated at the table, the meal placed before us and the blessing given, Mycroft Holmes told how a visit from

my wife to the Diogenes Club one evening in early December had resulted in the day's intricate staging. Mycroft said he had become so completely absorbed in preparing the trap for his brother that he inadvertently precipitated something of a scandal when his request for a disused handkerchief with the mark of the Prince of Wales from the King's private secretary caused a stir at Downing Street, and a reprimand from the Prime Minister!

He had begun describing with relish the unconventional method by which Wiggins, the leader of the Irregulars, had procured a bottle of sand from the pile outside the shop of the unsuspecting bookseller, when I interrupted.

"One moment, Mycroft. Perhaps your brother has, by now, worked out all the details himself, and would not be averse to sharing with us the explanation of how your great feat was accomplished?"

"I daresay you know him as well as I, Doctor!" Mycroft nodded at our guest before turning his attention to the food upon his plate. "Sherlock?"

"Why, thank you, Mycroft." My old friend wore a satisfied grin. "I believe I do possess all the threads of the little adventure that led me here, and if it pleases Mrs. Watson, I will do as the good Doctor suggests while the rest of the company feast upon this most succulent-looking duck, knowing that my brother will not hesitate to point out where I go wrong in spelling out 'The Case of the Disappearing Beaune'"—he paused to wag a cautionary forefinger at the now-unmufflered 'doorman' seated with the other Irregulars—"and no, not that *dog* bone you were on about!"

Once more we all laughed, and then the masterful and self-assured figure of Sherlock Holmes began to describe, in his crisp, didactic fashion, the various methods by which the grown-up men of the Baker

Street Irregulars and their wives, with the able assistance of Miss Kitty Winter and the estimable Shinwell Johnson, had enacted the elaborate stage play crafted by Mycroft Holmes in consultation with Inspector Lestrade—from the identification of the innocent bookseller as Professor Moriarty's criminal successor to the various cabs placed strategically about the streets of London ("knowing that my suspicious nature would require auxiliary drivers, of course!") and even the stationing of a coal lorry outside the Morland Hotel, where the costumed wives of the Irregulars sang, over and over, the Danish folk song they had memorized, until Holmes's appearance in the cab.

"But it was the almond that was a stroke of genius," Sherlock Holmes concluded, with evident respect for his brother's talents. "I was certain we were facing a plot against the entire Royal Family."

Mycroft shrugged his shoulders and demurred. "Suggested by a Danish emissary at the Diogenes Club when I picked his brain over lunch one day."

"Bravo, Mycroft. Bravo. There is, however, one thing I am not clear about. If I had not been seated on the east side of the cab when we drove past the Morland Hotel I never would have glimpsed the Danish flag and made the connection to the almond in the bottle. How did you know I would be sitting on that side?"

"Dr. Watson had assured me that in your heightened state of alarm you would enter the cab first, so we stationed the hansom across Parliament Street, knowing it would be positioned properly when the driver turned around and made his way up Tottenham Court Road. It was one of those peculiar habits of yours which Dr. Watson has witnessed over the years, and he was right!"

"Well done, Doctor," said Sherlock Holmes with some little feeling, and I blushed as Mycroft continued.

"Every movement was choreographed in advance, Sherlock, and every reaction of yours was anticipated, down to that scene in the cab with the old cap worn by Dr. Watson! But it was those Irregulars who made it all possible." Mycroft beamed across the table at the young men and their wives, then nodded at the man still wearing the red Santa Claus jacket. "Mr. Wiggins has a most pleasing tenor, wouldn't you agree, Sherlock?"

The Irregular who had led the Salvation Army choir now produced a white beard, placed it over his chin and took a modest bow as we all applauded.

"He does indeed, Mycroft." Sherlock Holmes fingered his glass of Beaune from the bottle that had been switched in his sitting room. "But to you, Wiggins, and the rest of the young men and women of the Irregulars—" Here he paused and studied each of their faces with a stern countenance that caused us all to take in our breath once more. "I'm sorry I trained you so well!"

Then he broke into a smile and raised his glass. "To the Irregulars!"

"The Irregulars!" we all toasted.

And again, we laughed—none more than Wiggins and his mates.

When the company had once again quieted, Sherlock Holmes made his final, and altogether softest and most sincere, toast.

To my wife.

"Madam, I thank you for opening your home to Mycroft and me on this blessed day. I shall never refuse your kindness again."

And he wouldn't.

Such were the true circumstances behind the most satisfying Christmas Day I would spend with Sherlock Holmes, and one of the best days of the many of all our years of friendship.

And I am happy to say that each year thereafter, even when he had left behind London and his life's work as England's greatest detective for a cottage upon the Sussex Downs to tend his bees and write his memoirs, Sherlock Holmes would attend our Christmas feast.

No invitation was ever necessary.

The End

Acknowledgements

This book owes its existence to David Marcum and my wife Nancy.

David is the superlative editor of MX Publishing's "New Sherlock Holmes" anthologies, and his call for Sherlock Holmes Christmas stories caught my eye soon after my first novel, *One Must Tell the Bees: Abraham Lincoln and the Final Education of Sherlock Holmes*, had been published. I thought it would be great fun—and a worthwhile challenge—to write a story on-demand and with the constraint that the story be consistent with "the canon," as Sherlockians call the original 56 Sherlock Holmes stories and novels written by Sir Arthur Conan Doyle.

That was no great constraint, of course. I had written *One Must Tell the Bees* with the utmost respect for the canon, although the tale of Holmes's coming to America during the final year of the Civil War raised eyebrows among purists who believe Holmes would have been far too young to have met Abraham Lincoln in 1864 and to have taken part in the manhunt for Lincoln's assassin, John Wilkes Booth, during April of 1865.

I heartily disagree, of course, and welcome the debate *One Must Tell the Bees* has stirred in the Sherlockian community as being healthy and entirely, well, Sherlockian.

In any case, I had great fun constructing *The Case of the Disappearing Beaune* in line with the canon, and, happily David not only accepted the story but he proved to possess a very deft touch as an editor, and it was published in the November 2021 MX Sherlock Holmes Christmas anthology.

I thank David for that.

But it was my wife Nancy who suggested *The Case of the Disappearing Beaune* could also stand on its own. I set about reassembling the team that had polished and produced *One Must Tell the Bees*: editor Beth Stein, whose infallible radar helped me vastly improve the Beaune storyline; proofreader Michael Mann, whose contribution went above and beyond fixing typos and grammatical errors; illustrator Robert Hunt, whose beautiful painting graces the cover; and the production team of Hannah Robertson at BooksFluent for the interior design. Finally, Ray Riethmeier, BSI, provided some very helpful last-minute corrections to the text. Hence, the novella you hold in your hands.

—J. L. Matthews

About the Author

J. Lawrence Matthews is the author of *One Must Tell the Bees: Abraham Lincoln and the Final Education of Sherlock Holmes*, a "tour de force" that brought Sherlock Holmes and Abraham Lincoln together for the first time. *The Case of the Disappearing Beaune* is his second novel. He has contributed fiction to the *New York Times* and *NPR's All Things Considered,* and is the author of three non-fiction books as Jeff Matthews, including *Pilgrimage to Omaha* (McGraw-Hill, 2010).